ROSE and the NIGHTINGALE

Other Dragonfly Books you will enjoy

The Angel and the Soldier Boy by Peter Collington
Manhattan by Jean Christian Knaff
Christmas by Jan Pieńkowski
A New Coat for Anna by Harriet Ziefert

ROSE and the NIGHTINGALE

INGA MOORE

Dragonfly Books · Alfred A. Knopf
New York

A DRAGONFLY BOOK PUBLISHED BY ALFRED A. KNOPF, INC.

Library of Congress Cataloging-in-Publication Data
Moore, Inga.
Rose and the nightingale / Inga Moore.
p.   cm.
A Dragonfly book.
Summary: Rose, a poor baker's girl, sacrifices her hard-earned savings
out of pity for a caged nightingale and gains the attention of the
handsome boy for whom she had saved in the first place.
ISBN 0-679-80197-9
[1. Nightingales—Fiction.] I. Title.
PZ7.M7846Ro   1990
[E]—dc20   89-24429
CIP
AC

First Dragonfly edition: June 1990
Manufactured in the United States of America
1   2   3   4   5   6   7   8   9   10

ROSE and the NIGHTINGALE

Rose was a hardworking baker's girl. All day long her arms were pale with flour. But though she worked hard, her wages were low, and Rose was poor as poor could be.

Her home was a drafty little attic above the bakery, and all she had to wear were two plain smocks.

Now, Rose was in love with a handsome boy. Each day she would see him ride past the bakery on a horse as white as milk. He wore a cocked hat and a cloak which fell from his shoulders like a raven's wings. His jacket was velvet, and lace tumbled from his collar and frothed at his cuff. At his heels shone spurs of silver.

Rose would stand shyly by the door to watch him, feeling so plain in her smock.

Often she stood there. Never, never did he look her way.

Then, one day, Rose saw a very pretty dress in a shop window.

"You look like a princess!" cried the dressmaker when Rose went inside and tried it on.

"Cash or account?"

Of course, Rose had no money at all.

The dressmaker, who was a kind woman, packed the dress into a box and put it to one side. She allowed Rose six months in which to pay.

So Rose began to scrimp and save. She worked longer hours for extra wages, climbing wearily into her bed at night only to rise again early next morning.

Weeks turned into months, and pennies to shillings, until, nearly six months later, she had saved almost enough. Just a few pence more and the dress was hers.

Payday came round again. Rose waited excitedly for her wages. She was serving in the shop, counting the hours until closing time, when in through the door came a peddler. He was carrying a cage. Fluttering helplessly inside was a nightingale.

"It's from Persia, miss." (In fact, he had caught it in a wood not a mile away.) "And only two guineas."

When Rose saw the nightingale her heart was torn in two.

Rose ran upstairs to fetch her savings.

"I'm afraid I'm a few pence short," she told the peddler, handing the money over. The peddler didn't seem to mind. He ran out the door as fast as his crooked legs would carry him.

Rose carried the nightingale upstairs to her attic.

She opened the window. Then she opened the cage door. Out flew the nightingale into the sunlight.

But it didn't fly away at once; it flew into a tree, where it began to sing, filling the air with its beautiful voice.

Rose leant from her window, enchanted.

At that moment, who should ride by but the handsome boy.

Such was the beauty of the nightingale's song that he drew rein to listen.

Searching for the bird, he saw Rose at her window.

Eventually the nightingale flew away. Rose went downstairs to finish her work.

Night fell and she was scrubbing still, trying hard not to think of the pretty dress. But one by one her tears began to fall.

Suddenly there was a knock at the door. Rose dried her eyes, wondering who it could be.

It was the handsome boy.